AF480096

THE
MEAN
Sewing Machine

THE
MEAN
Sewing Machine

Mia Oliver

The Mean Sewing Machine
Copyright © 2022
First Edition
Written and Illustrated by: Mia Oliver
Edited by: Heather Oliver
ISBN 9798353499176

This Book is dedicated to:

To my mom and her sewing machine.

One day there was a
sewing machine at Ms.
Heather's house.

The sewing machine
was mean.

Ms. Heather went to her
sewing machine
and a shiver went down
her spine.

Despite the shiver, she
began to sew.

Except, the electronic
sewing machine
did not let her sew.

It stopped working
and beeped at her
over and over again.

Frustrated, she walked
away.

6

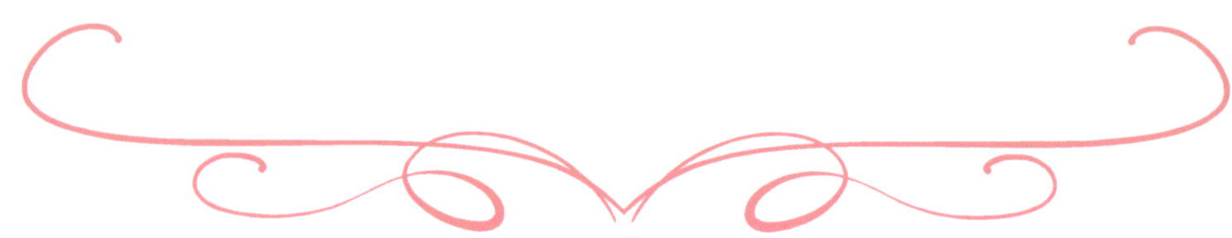

But, Ms. Heather did not give up easily.

The more she sewed, the meaner the sewing machine got!

The sewing machine beeped and took the thread out of it's needle.

Ms. Heather was
FURIOUS!

She stomped away and
started researching
other sewing machines
on the internet.

Stubbornly, Ms. Heather came back to the sewing machine and said,
"This is your last chance! If you don't work, I will replace you!"

The sewing machine gasped at the thought of a life without sewing.

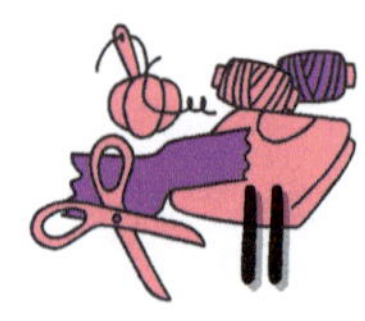

12

The mean sewing machine put the thread back in the needle and stopped beeping.

Together they worked hard and finished the sewing project. Ms. Heather never had to replace her sewing machine.

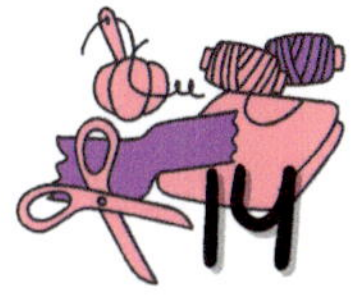

The End

About the Author:

Mia Oliver is an 8 year old girl who is aspiring to be an author and is making her dreams come true. Mia has a vivid imagination and loves to bring her visions to life through pictures and words. She lives in Florida with her mom, dad, and two brothers. She enjoys sewing, practicing Juijitsu, crafting and spending time with family and friends.